alōōza

ounds of Celebration!

By Teresa Domnauer

School Specialty. Publishing

Text Copyright © 2006 School Specialty Publishing. Farkle McBride Character © 2000 by John Lithgow. Farkle McBride Illustration © 2000 by C.F. Payne.

Library of Congress Cataloging-in-Publication Data is on file with the publisher.

Send all inquiries to:
School Specialty Publishing
8720 Orion Place
Columbus, OH 43240-2111

ISBN 0-7696-4233-0

1 2 3 4 5 6 7 8 9 10 PHXBK 10 09 08 07 06 05

Table of Contents

"Happy Birthday to You"

Have you ever been
to a birthday party?
If so, you probably heard
"Happy Birthday to You."
This famous song was written
by two sisters.
At first, the words said
"Good Morning to All."
But the words to the song
have changed.
Now, we sing
"Happy Birthday to You!"

Farkle Fact

In 1893, Mildred and Patty Hill wrote this song
for the children at the school where they both taught.

"Pomp and Circumstance"

A special song is played
when someone graduates.
This song is called
"Pomp and Circumstance."
Sir Edward Elgar wrote this music.
When a college gave
Sir Edward an award,
the musicians played
"Pomp and Circumstance."
Now, it is played
at most **graduation ceremonies**.

Farkle Fact

Elgar wrote "Pomp and Circumstance" for the crowning
of King Edward VII in England.

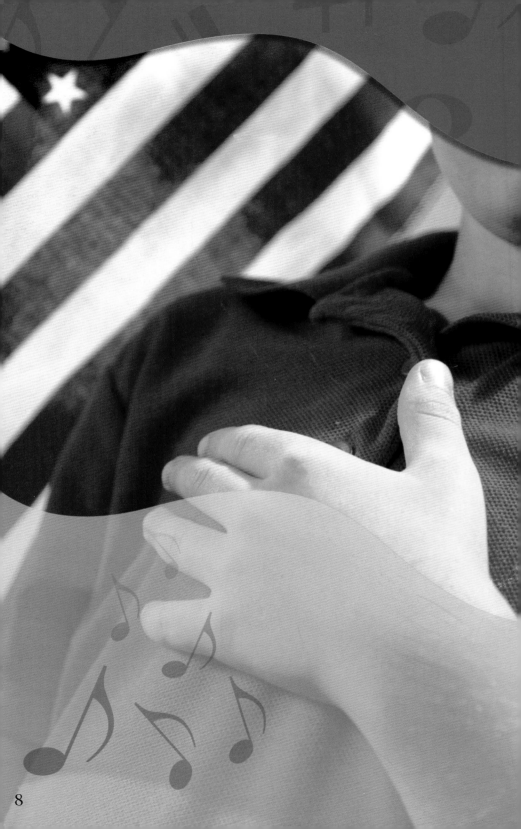

"The Star-Spangled Banner"

Many countries have a national **anthem**. This is a song that is very special to a country and its people. "The Star-Spangled Banner" is the national anthem of the United States. It was written by Francis Scott Key. He wrote the song during the War of 1812.

Farkle Fact

Key wrote this song after seeing the American flag still waving after battle. The song tells how proud he felt about our country's bravery.

"Here Comes the Bride"

At weddings,
you might hear
"Here Comes the Bride."
This song plays when the bride
walks down the aisle.
It was written by
composer Richard Wagner.
He wrote the song for an **opera**.
Today, it is played at many weddings.

Farkle Fact

Another song often played at weddings is "The Wedding March." This song is played at the end of the wedding.

Songs for Holidays

There are special songs that people sing on holidays. You might sing "Jingle Bells" on Christmas Day. You might sing "I Have a Little Dreidel" during Hanukkah. People sing special songs for Kwanzaa, Passover, St. Patrick's Day, Valentine's Day, and many other holidays!

Farkle Fact

The music to "Silent Night" was written on Christmas Eve in 1818. Franz Gruber finished writing the music just in time to be played at the midnight service!

"Auld Lang Syne"

For New Year's,
people often sing a song
called "Auld Lang Syne."
The song comes from
a Scottish folk song.
Sometimes, people don't understand
the song's old-fashioned words.
It is about remembering friends
and happy times.

Farkle Fact

The poet Robert Burns is thought to have written
the words to this song. In Scotland, "Auld Lang Syne"
is sung every year on his birthday, an event known as
"Burns' Night."

Patriotic Songs

Patriotic songs show people's love for their country. In the United States, people sing patriotic songs on July 4th, Memorial Day, Veteran's Day, and Flag Day. In America, some patriotic songs are "This Land Is Your Land" and "You're a Grand Old Flag."

Farkle Fact

"America the Beautiful" was written by Katharine Lee Bates in 1893. She wrote the song during a trip to the mountains of Colorado.

"Taps"

"Taps" is a song played on a single bugle. It was written by General Daniel Adams Butterfield in 1862 as a **tribute** to soldiers. The slow sound of "Taps" says it is the end of the day. It tells soldiers to turn out the lights. "Taps" is also played at sad times, such as funerals.

Farkle Fact

The short, moving **melody** of "Taps" has only 24 notes.

"Reveille"

If you have gone to camp,
you might know
the tune of "Reveille."
"Reveille" is another song
played on a single bugle.
It is played early in the morning.
It signals that it is time
to rise and shine!

Farkle Fact

The word *reveille* comes from a French word that means "to waken."

"Bugler's Dream"

Have you ever watched
the Olympics on television?
If so, you might know
"Bugler's Dream."
This tune features
a **fanfare** of trumpets.
The music was written
by Leo Arnaud in 1958.
It was not written for the Olympics.
"Bugler's Dream" is part of a larger
piece of music.

Farkle Fact

"Bugler's Dream" was first played during the 1968
Winter Olympics, which were held in France.

"Hail to the Chief"

The President
of the United States
has his own special song.
When he appears in public,
"Hail to the Chief" is played.
The music was written to go
with a poem called "Lady of the Lake."
The poem was written
by Sir Walter Scott in 1810.
It was set to music by James Sanderson.
Today, "Hail to the Chief" is known
as the President's theme song.

Farkle Fact

"Hail to the Chief" was first played during a ceremony celebrating George Washington's birthday.

Parade Music

You may have seen
a marching band at a parade.
Its members carry instruments
and play music while they march.
Many colleges and high schools
have marching bands
that play **marches**.
Marches have very strong beats.
Some marching band members
do not play instruments.
Instead, they carry flags, twirl batons,
or dance.

Farkle Fact

The marching band at Purdue University in Indiana
has almost 400 members! It is known as the world's
largest marching band.

Songs That Celebrate Faith

Music is a part of many
religious services.
Often, worshippers sing
hymns together.
A hymn is a song of praise.
One very famous hymn
is "Amazing Grace."
It was written by an English priest
named John Newton.
He wrote the song after living through
a terrible storm at sea.

Farkle Fact

"Amazing Grace" is very popular. There have been over
450 different versions of this song recorded!

Vocabulary

anthem–a patriotic song. *Many countries have a national anthem.*

celebration–an event that honors something. *We had a celebration for my mother and father's anniversary.*

ceremony–an event that honors a special occasion. *The family attended Juan's graduation ceremony.*

composer–a person who writes music. *Beethoven was a great composer.*

fanfare–the sound of trumpets. *The fanfare sounded as the race began.*

graduation–a ceremony that celebrates when someone finishes school or studies. *We went to my sister's high school graduation.*

hymn–a song of praise. *We sang a hymn at church.*

march–a piece of music with a strong beat that is created to go along with marching. *The band played a march by John Philip Sousa.*

melody–musical notes that make a pleasing sound. *"Happy Birthday" has a familiar melody.*

opera–a play in which the words are sung. *We went to see an opera in New York City.*

patriotic–the feeling of love for one's country. *We sang patriotic songs on the Fourth of July.*

tribute–an acknowledgment of gratitude, respect, or admiration. *The award was a tribute to her hard work.*

Think About It!

1. Who wrote the song "Happy Birthday To You"? Why was it written?

2. Where might you hear the tune "Bugler's Dream

3. What is the name of the President's theme song

4. What does "Taps" signal?

5. What is the song "Auld Lang Syne" about?

The Story and You!

1. What special songs do you and your family sing on holidays?

2. Can you think of a patriotic song that you have sung?

3. Have you ever heard the sound of a bugle? Where?

4. Think of a special celebration that you attended where music was played. What kind of music was it?

5. Do all songs make you feel happy? Do some songs make you feel sad?